"WATSON!"

AND OTHER UNAUTHORIZED SHERLOCK HOLMES PASTICHES, PARODIES, AND SEQUELS

"WATSON!"
AND OTHER UNAUTHORIZED SHERLOCK HOLMES PASTICHES, PARODIES, AND SEQUELS

by

CAPTAIN A.E. DINGLE

G.F. FORREST

BRET HARTE

O. HENRY

JOHN KENDRICK BANGS

WILDSIDE PRESS

CONTENTS

"WATSON!"

by Captain A.E. Dingle

"**W**ATSON, my dear fellow, this inaction is maddening. I am *ennuied*," drawled a lanky, cadaverous individual reclining lumpishly in a long deck chair, a black cigar in his teeth, his brows drawn down, and his fingertips touching in approved Sherlockian fashion. A ripple of mirth passes around the small circle of which he formed the centre, and his expression darkened in outward resentment.

The man addressed as Watson glanced at the amused ones with a faint smile on his own face and replied indifferently, "Better take a dose of dope, my dear Holmes. The steward uncorks a rippin' brand of Scotch. Shall I call him?"

Holmes unfolded himself out of the chair without a reply and stalked away in the direction of the smoking room.

"He's on the scent!" chuckled a fiery-haired youngster.

"That's a scent you all can follow!" replied a merry-eyed girl, seizing the red one and dragging him off to play shuffleboard. Watson remained in his chair, and behind lowered lids his eyes glittered shrewdly.

Percy Anstruther's big steam yacht *Vagrant* never went to sea without a happy, careless party of youth aboard.

Percy himself was of the type dubbed porcine. Finding himself tremendously wealthy quite early in life, mainly by dint of ignoring the Golden Rule and playing up the Rule of Three — which he interpreted to mean, one for the firm — of which he was head — and two for Percy Anstruther — holding no scruples which might prevent profits accruing through some such idiocy as consideration for others, he soon decided, on retiring, that a steam yacht was the thing to gain him entry into the society of the exclusive set he desired to adorn. Percy knew enough to refrain from attempting the impossible; he paid high salaries, not wages, to the best of secretaries, the cunningest of chefs, the very paragon of stewards, and he possessed that native shrewdness which prevented him offending by any vulgarity of speech in select company, no matter how free he might be among his own kind. No amount of shrewdness could warn him of the bad taste, or inadvisability, of loading himself with costly, bizarre jewelry. He saw ladies and gentlemen of the class he envied, each wearing such gems as they possessed when occasion demanded. In his small mind there was only one reason for their not wearing more — the lack of possession; only one reason for limiting the times of wearing what they had — fear of losing them. And since neither fear of losing them nor limited possession applied to himself, Percy Anstruther's fat fingers were ever loaded with flawless diamonds, his fat neck glowed from the fires within a great single ruby in his scarf, his fat watch fob scintillated like a cluster of stars against his fat little paunch.

"I've got 'em, why shouldn't I sport 'em?" he had demanded many times in answer to suggestions from his friends. "I can afford to wear 'em, and the crook isn't born who'll take 'em away from your Uncle Percy. No, sir!"

Which all brings us back to Holmes and Watson; for it was the long, lean, cadaverous Holmes who first expressed entire agreement with Percy's ideas on the subject of fashion in gems. They had met, and become acquainted, at the great Casino of Ocean View, off which the Vagrant lay anchored while her owner and his guests disported in a dance or two, a turn or so at the wheel, or a little chopping, according to individual taste. Percy, furthermore, strongly desired to become acquainted with somebody who would accept his hospitality without making him see and feel that he became a debtor by receiving the honor of the present company. He was gratified by the celerity with which he attained his object. There could be no doubt regarding the desirability of Mr. Holmes or his friend Watson. Those names appeared on the register of their hotel, and by them they were known and introduced to Percy by the croupier of the roulette table. There could be no cavilling at friends secured through such a sponsor. And, best of all, they quite certainly did not seek his acquaintance merely to have a finger in his pocket-book, for they politely insisted upon buying wine themselves; and their taste was proven when they ordered a brand which Percy always hesitated about, though he knew it was quite the thing, simply because he wasn't sure how to pronounce the name.

"I say, you chaps must come for a cruise with me," he had said eagerly at the third bottle.

"The ocean's rather a bore, old man, but perhaps we could endure it for a few days, ah, Watson?" Holmes had replied in a drawl which seemed incongruous with the sharpness of his big, steady eyes.

"Oh, just for a week, perhaps," Watson had conceded, with similar lack of eagerness, and the thing was done. They vacated their hotel that same day; the *Vagrant* steamed just beyond the blue skyline in the cool evening.

WITH a young party on board, it was inevitable that Holmes should speedily acquire the name of "Sherlock." For Dr. Watson to be dubbed "Doctor" followed as naturally as night follows day. At first they mildly resented it, although, queerly enough, Holmes rather deserved it than otherwise, for he was forever reading the detective books in the yacht's well-stocked library, and he could easily be led on to expound the methods of the famous sleuth of fiction. But soon they accepted the titles bestowed on them, and gradually Percy, seeing the fun the others got out of the little pleasantry, and seeing that his new guests suffered nothing actually by it, fell into the mood himself, and often cast out bait in the hope of getting Holmes into a tangle of explanations over some really trivial circumstance. Such as the time, for instance, when the crew's cook, who looked after the fowls carried to supply the owner's table with fresh eggs, reported the best layer missing, and the boatswain, at the same time, pointed out to the chief officer chicken tracks up the side of the freshly painted smokestack.

"You let the bloomin' chicken loose yourself while washing down decks," was the mate's emphatic decision. "You scared her trying to chase her back, and the bally thing flew up against the funnel before she volplaned overboard. You want to be more careful, bo'sun."

But Percy, urged on by his young friends, suggested to Holmes that there might be another solution to the missing chicken mystery. Holmes placed the tips of his long, white fingers together, drew down his brows, and nodded sagaciously. From the stokehold grating came the merry whistle of a happy fireman whose spirits were proof against the discomfort of his work. A windlass clanked, and two firemen just off duty drew up a can of ashes and dumped them down the lower-deck shute; from the galley door a sculleryman emerged, staggering under the kitchen garbage pail. Both containers discharged their waste into the blue sea at once, and tigerishly Holmes darted to the rail and keenly scanned the floating refuse. Then he resumed his chair, lighted a huge briar pipe filled with strong plug, and placed his finger-tips together again, while Percy Anstruther and the merry band of youngsters waited for his next utterance.

"You are right, Mr. Anstruther," he said crisply. "There is another, very different answer to that seemingly simple riddle of the chicken."

"Oh, surely you have not solved the mystery so soon?" protested Percy. His young friends giggled.

"My chain is almost complete, sir," Holmes replied.

"You hear that peculiar whistle emanating from the fireroom? I dare say it is the first time you have noticed it. But I, who note the meanest trifles, can assure you that there has been, is, method in that whistle. Where are the poultry pens? Right beside the stokehold ventilators, are they not? Very well. The messmate of the whistling fireman slyly opens the cage, the whistler pipes up a cunning note, the chicken creeps out, the cage is once more fastened, and the miscreant who opened and closed it darts below to join his fellow criminal. The whistling goes on, the poor deluded chicken follows it, and now it takes on the quality of ventriloquism. It seems to emanate from the funnel. The silly fowl walks up the smokestack, the fumes overcome it when it gets to the rim, and it falls down into the hands of the hungry pair waiting for its advent, singed and cooked ready to devour. That, gentlemen, is the solution of an apparent mystery. Quite simple."

A roar of merriment pealed out across the sea, and Holmes appeared annoyed.

"Fine!" laughed Percy, with the conscious superiority of having discovered a palpable flaw. "But tell us, old chap, how these awful criminals got the chicken out of the furnace? It would be burned up long before it reached the bottom of that chimney."

"You may amuse yourselves unravelling that point, gentlemen. I will give you a tip, though. I stepped to the rail just now. You imagined I did so idly, or simply to knock out my pipe. It was not so. I examined the refuse thrown over at that instant. Feathers, some burnt, some whole, floated away on a mass of ashes. It is the trifles which count in detecting crime. Now, Watson, I think we will investigate a rumor that the steward was seen breaking out a new case of Scotch this morning."

There was a medley of voices in the group he left. Some actually wondered if he really believed in his own deep cunning, since he was never seen to smile even while expounding his most outlandish notions. Others were only disgusted. There were two who warned Percy without reserve that before the cruise was up he would be touched for money by the Sherlockian Holmes and his friend Watson.

"Oh, I don't think that," objected Percy. "He's rather idiotic, of course, but I think the chap's only fooling himself. They're both gentlemen, anyway, and we're having some fun with them."

"Why not let us make up a real mystery, Percy?"

"Oh, goody!" cried a merry-eyed girl, dancing joyously. "Oh, let's! You can have a tremendous robbery, or something, and have all the clues point to all of us, and all of us have an alibi, and you can scatter my hair-pins and combs about, and —"

"That's the identical scheme!" chuckled Percy, shaking like a jelly in his mirth. "Let's dope out a plot."

"Presently!" interjected the red-headed youth, intensely. "Here's the Watson chap. Not a word!"

Watson strolled along the deck, having left Holmes in the smoking room, and he wore a grimace of mingled boredom and contempt. He glanced around the little group inquisitively, then addressed Percy.

"Holmes begins to irritate one, doesn't he, Anstruther? A little of his nonsense is amusing; too much is sickening. I wonder what he'd do if faced with a real case. Sometimes I think he's really keen on scientific investigation of problems, at others I feel disgusted at his childishness. The chicken twaddle, for instance."

Percy hesitated for a minute, then, smiling fatly in justification of his resolve, he said.

"I say, Watson, you must be a thought-reader. When you came along we were discussing playing a little joke on your friend to see how far he would dig into a real puzzle. You won't mind if we keep you out of it, will you? Might drop him a hint, you know, and spoil —"

"Not at all," replied Watson quickly. "Make your plans and start him going. I'll have my fun looking on, I assure you. I hope you concoct a real mystery, though, with something far deeper than vanishing poultry as a motive. Good luck."

The first outcome of a long and close secret confabulation was the sudden increase of Percy's jewelled embellishments. That evening at dinner he simply blazed with light from gorgeous gems, and in place of his customary offering of big, sleek Cuban cigars in a handsome snake-skin case after dinner, he preferred still choicer weeds in an amazing gold case on both sides of which his monogram leaped out at one in diamonds. Then, under pretence of showing the men some intimate curiosities, he took them into his great stateroom where, obviously through oversight, a stout cash box stood open on his table, crammed to the top with bank notes of high denomination.

"Confound that man of mine!" he exclaimed, closing the box, but leaving it on the table. "He's always leaving valuables about as if they were pebbles."

While exhibiting the trivial curiosities he had brought the men in to see, he shot keen side-glances at Holmes, and chuckled shakily as he led the way out to the after deck, omitting to reprimand his valet, however, for his carelessness.

"It's a gorgeous night," he remarked, when the space under the awnings resounded with tuneful music from an excellent machine.

"Let's have a bit of dancing, hey, folks?"

In the quietest hour of the most silent watch, about two o'clock in the morning, the yacht rang with sounds of dire mis-happening. A pistol shot shattered the stillness on deck, a heavy splash was heard over the side, and in a minute the decks were alive with alarmed seaman and excited officers; a huddle of sleepy guests milled about each other in well feigned panic. Watson was there, as panicky as the rest; and Holmes, true to his assumed character, took up the burden of discovering the meaning of that midnight alarm.

"Where is Mr. Anstruther?" he demanded, peering around like a scrawny hawk. "Find him, steward. Fancy him sleeping through such a racket! He's getting far too fat."

While Watson looked on in silence from the companionway door, and a little giggling group nudged each other delightedly, Holmes flashed a pocket torch about the decks and rails. On hands and knees at times, he nosed along waterways and peering overside into the silken blackness of the smooth sea. Presently he brought forth a huge magnifying glass, and the red-headed youth laughed outright. The sound seemed creepy in the darkness and quiet, broken before only by swish of water and that flickering circle of light from Holmes' torch. But the steward's sudden appearance and agitated announcement diverted attention again.

"Mr. Anstruther's — Oh, his room, it's horrid!"

Prepared as they were for such an announcement, it required all their self-control to prevent the conspirators uttering little gasps of sheer suspense, so vivid was the steward's terror. Watson glanced keenly toward the absorbed figure of Holmes, who was scrutinizing the steward pitilessly, every inch of the man's outward aspect coming under the inspection.

"That will do, my man," snapped Holmes at length. "You may show us the way to Mr. Anstruther's stateroom. Come, Watson, I may need you." The steward led the way trembling, and the muffled giggling burst forth again as the youthful jesters saw the Sherlockian one tumbling into the trap they had set for him. All the details of the plot had been left to Anstruther, and they were sure he had done a good piece of work, for he had outlined most of what he intended to do, but none had anticipated the perfection of theatrical setting which seemed to leap out at them through the door of Percy's room.

"Ooh!" cried the merry-eyed girl, and shrank back with fright which was more than half real. Her companions too, playing out their hands, peeped inside, drew back, gasped and stared in simulated terror. Watson looked in, then stepped inside, his ruddy face wearing an enigmatical expression. Holmes alone maintained an utterly expressionless air as he waved everyone back from the threshold and took from his pocket a tape measure.

Well indeed had Percy done his part. The bed was upset, and the coverings strewed the carpet. One curtain flew loose through the wide porthole, the other hung by one hook, torn in halves. The table and writing desk in a corner were bare; the drawers, both hanging open almost out of the slides, lay empty. The stout cash box was on the floor, empty but one forlorn note of small denomination lay pinched under one corner of it. Across the room, near the bed, which was a four-poster and not a bunk, was a woman's hair comb, broken; a yard away lay a pyjama button, still a yard further a red and green grass bath slipper, obviously far too small for Percy to have ever worn. And, stabbing the dim light like a spear, a great red smear ran from a dark stain on the bed-head clear up to and through the open port.

Watson stepped over and touched the red smear with a finger, smelling it and peering at it under a light globe. A queer curl wreathed his lips, and he glanced curiously at Holmes who was on his knees with tape and lens. Afterward, when talking over the events of that night, some of the young men recalled that queer glance of Watson's, and remembered, too, that he contrived to get into the foreground quite as much as Holmes, yet without in the slightest degree seeming to want to. Anyhow, in all the after pictures of that night which rose up before any of the guests, the short, heavy figure of Watson loomed as large as the long, thin, stooping figure of Holmes.

"What's happened, d'you think?" whispered somebody. The merry-eyed girl giggled hysterically, and rejoined, "Give Mr. Holmes time. Don't you all see there's been a horrid crime committed, and that poor Percy has vanished? Don't breathe. You may disturb something, mayn't they, Mr. Holmes?"

For answer Holmes suddenly appeared before the little group in the door, his eyes ablaze.

He seemed to arrive from the other side of the room without, motion, like a shadow; and without warning he plunged his hand into the tumbled mass of shining hair over the girl's startled eyes. In the other hand he held the broken parts of the hair comb he had picked up from the floor.

"Same color," he muttered, matching comb with hair. "Where is your comb, miss?"

Confronted with the very thing she had suggested herself, the girl looked less happy than she had expected. Confusion seized upon her, and her saucy tongue failed her. She stammered, sheepishly enough, "That is it. I er — I lent it to Percy to, er — to —"

"That is all, thank you," Holmes interrupted her sharply. "I will ask for you when I require your statement. You may retire." A tiny murmur of protest rippled around at sight of the girl's crestfallen air as she turned away toward her own room; but then the hugeness of the joke struck all concerned, and they crowded close to hear what was coming next.

Holmes closely examined the carpet, the bed, the curtains; he even measured the length and breadth of the red smear on the side panel. He sniffed at some dust he scraped up, he struck his head through the porthole and peered up and down, fore and aft, like a raw-necked vulture seeking prey. Then, stepping to the centre again, he looked for a moment at the faces before him and at the red and green bath slipper. Suddenly he went to his knees before the red-headed youth and forcibly lifted his right foot knee-high. He flung aside the leather Romeo the young man wore and clamped the grass slipper to the foot.

"H'm! You, too, I shall know where to find when I need you," he remarked. "You may retire, sir; and I warn you that this very serious occurrence may lead into unpleasant places. If you wish to tell me anything, you may do so in the morning. That is all, thank you."

Now he held out the pyjama button, scanning the sleeping suits before him. One jacket lacked a button, and one only. Like a tiger Holmes sprang before the wearer, clapped the button to the vacant place, and glared terribly into the young fellow's face. "B-but, Holmes, it isn't the same pattern!" giggled another bystander, scarcely able to talk for repressed mirth.

"Married?" Holmes jerked out abruptly to the man who lacked a button.

"Surely," laughed the youngster, recovering his nerve.

"Pattern doesn't matter then," was the unexpectedly sophisticated reply. "You will be called in the morning, sir. That will do."

"Say, Holmes," put in the last onlooker, who, except for Watson, alone remained unspotted by suspicion. "I don't lack a shoe, nor a button, nor even a comb. Can't you discover some clue which indicates me as the brutal murderer?" There was a keen note of sarcasm in the man's suggestion. Holmes looked at him gravely.

"I shall permit nothing to escape my notice which bears on this monstrous mystery," he said. "Place your left hand here, please."

With excessive care he pressed the man's hand down into the nap of the thick carpet, and scrutinized the edges through his powerful lens; then released the man and told him to go, but, like the rest, to hold himself ready to be questioned.

"Meanwhile," remarked Holmes, "we shall turn in toward some port. This is a matter for the regular police, to whom I hope to be able to deliver the criminal."

"Sure you can't find something which incriminates Watson?" gurgled the young fellow just released. "This is such a scream it would be a shame to keep him out of it."

"You will kindly keep your witticisms for a more suitable moment, sir," was the dry retort, and the guest departed, leaving Watson gazing thoughtfully at the stooping back of Holmes.

"My dear Watson," the sleuth said presently, "pray ring for the steward." The steward answered the bell, and Holmes told him, without turning around, to go and order the captain to change the course for the nearest port, and to notify him immediately which port it would be. In answer, the captain appeared in person, and a very angry, irritable person he was. He opened fire at once on the sleuth.

"What's the meaning of this?" he demanded warmly. "Why am I not called in to be consulted about this? And who are you, to order me into port, I'd like to know. Where's the owner?"

"Mr. Anstruther has disappeared, captain. There has been some foul play. That is why I suggest running into port —"

"And this is the first I hear of it!" bellowed the captain. "Shooting goes on aboard my ship, somebody tells me my owner has gone, and I'm not asked for an opinion but told to run —"

"Just a moment, captain," Watson put in quietly; "I will explain a lot to you if you'll give me a moment outside. There has been mischief, certainly, but not so serious as might be. Come, let Holmes continue his investigation. I'll tell you about it."

He led the mollified skipper out to his own roomy cabin, and Holmes flashed a look of appreciation after them as he shut the door.

An expectant party gathered about the table at breakfast in the morning, for daylight brought back all the brightness of the farce which night and its gloom had almost made to seem like tragedy. They awaited Holmes, who presently appeared looking haggard and pale after an obviously sleepless night. He crushed up a white pellet and stirred it into his coffee, which he drank before eating anything; then coldly, and with an incisiveness worthy of a graver situation, he plunged into a bald recital of his discoveries and decision. On deck, listening through the skylight, a gleeful yacht captain chuckled hugely, slapping his leg, utterly reconciled to the temporary loss of his employer.

"We shall be in port in a few hours now," Holmes began. "The culprit in this brazen piece of villainy will be taken ashore then, I promise you. You all heard the shot in the night, and —"

"How about the shoes and buttons and other haberdashery?" grinned the red-headed youth maliciously.

"I shall come to that, my young friend," replied Holmes, glaring fiercely. "You heard the shot, I believe. You all saw the scene of the crime —"

"That shot was on deck!"

"The scene of the crime," the sleuth proceeded as if no interruption had been offered, "and even my friend Watson could discern the obvious signs of violence there. You saw the odd slipper, the pyjama button, the broken comb, and the gory smear on the wall. Now there is one chance remaining for the guilty one to make reparation, and thereby perhaps gain leniency. I shall run over the facts, and on our arrival in port I shall summon the police to take the criminal, unless meanwhile he confesses.

"Now that slipper would fit only a child or a woman. That button might have come from a lounge pillow. The comb could easily have been picked up broken somewhere else and dropped in the cabin by the owner himself. I have some little skill in reading signs, and I say that pistol shot was fired out through a porthole, sounding thus as if it were on deck; the slipper is one of a heap of about fifty pairs of all sizes, kept by Mr. Anstruther for the use of guests who may have forgotten to bring bath shoes. The button assuredly came from the cushion in Anstruther's own arm chair, and the comb was probably dropped by him when he returned from the deck."

"Why, Holmes, you might be accusing Percy himself!" roared the party in mirth. Then, realizing suddenly that they ought to wear more of an air of gravity, since Percy was apparently murdered in his own yacht, and they were all more or less under suspicion, their faces fell, and they leaned closer to Holmes in deep attention.

"Making due allowance for youth and frivolity," Holmes proceeded coldly, "I will bear with you. Here is a tip, which you may find useful. Pray try to assist the course of justice, rather than hinder it because you do not see things as I see them. You would find the assassin and thief? Very well then. Look for a person of this description: A tall, lean man, rather stout, and about five feet eight inches high; he is florid and pale of complexion, and wears a number seven or number ten shoe. On one hand he has a crooked finger, which he can straighten whenever he wants to."

As one man the party got up from the table, and on every face was a sneer. They had expected something far better than this, else Percy would surely never have submitted to many hours of discomfort in order to play out the jest. The merry-eyed girl lingered behind to state, forcefully, her opinion.

"Mr. Holmes, I think you are a beast! If you are such an idiot as your silly words seem to indicate, you should at least have decency enough to refrain from uttering such nonsense at a time like this!"

She flirted out, and a slow, deep smile overspread Holmes' lean face as she disappeared. The captain, on deck, turned away to face a stammering, pop-eyed steward at his elbow.

"Mr. Anstruther, sir! He's down —"

"S-sh!" the skipper warned the man sharply. "Keep your mouth shut, steward. This is all right. Don't say a word."

"B-but, sir, he looks —"

"I tell you it's all right. It's a game he's playing. Keep quiet, I tell you."

Watson was having a similarly difficult time persuading his fellow guests to let the joke go on a little longer. They were, to a man and girl, for seeking out Percy and telling him it was useless to remain in hiding any longer.

"Why, Watson, it's too darned silly to be funny," cried the red-headed one. "It's simply idiotic to let old Percy sweat himself sick down in some dark hold just to draw this faker Holmes. I never heard such rubbish, even from half-witted kids."

"Don't spoil it," Watson advised quietly. "I know Holmes rather better than you, and I tell you he's only trying to scare you off while he makes out a case. If you leave him alone, say until we get to port, he'll have something amusing to tell you, even if it is all wrong. At any rate it will be a logical sequence of points comparing perfectly with all the clues."

"But how about poor old Percy?"

"I'll see him myself. He'll be agreeable, I know, since he arranged the joke himself. I'll take him down some wine and see what else he wants."

"Oh, then you know where he's hiding? He didn't tell us."

"I know, yes. Just keep quiet and watch awhile. You'll have something truly interesting to talk about soon, I promise you."

The yacht ran into harbor before noon, and as she steamed up the sail-dotted bay Holmes came on deck in town clothes. Every eye fastened on him, and smiles were carefully concealed.

"I am going on shore to bring the police, gentlemen," he stated sharply. "There is little time, but still time enough, for the culprit to reveal himself."

He turned away and stood at the rail. Behind him muffled giggles and chuckles broke out, and the merry-eyed girl chirped recklessly, "Oh yes, let him go! It'll be bully sport seeing the real police tear his silly old theories to rags."

Holmes seemed to notice nothing that was said, but presently the steward appeared absolutely dripping with the perspiration of fear, and in a moment all was changed from farce to earnest.

"Captain!" the man yelled to the bridge, "I've found Mr. Anstruther, and he's hurt! He ain't fooling, no, sir! He's been tied —"

Watson stepped forward, laid a hand on Holmes' arm coolly, and jabbed a pistol muzzle into his ribs. He faced the group with a smile.

"The steward is right, gentlemen. You thought to play a joke, but Long Holmes here turned it into a real game. That is, he almost succeeded. But I have been keeping tabs on him for a long time, and I've got him now with the goods. Yes, I'm a detective. You might see after Mr. Anstruther. I shall come back and report to him as soon as I've placed my prisoner in safety."

Holmes twisted his neck and glared down at Watson with murderous eyes; but the smaller man kept his pistol pressed to the other's side until the yacht docked, then put it into his pocket, warned his prisoner, and marched him ashore and into a taxicab.

Percy was brought up from the darksome depths of the storerooms, blinking and furious, but more than a little frightened. He shook a fat, abrased fist after the disappearing taxicab when the captain told him who was in it, and launched into a feverish recital of his adventures.

"By the Great Horn Spoon!" he gabbled, reddening up like a turkey's wattles. "That chap's smart, but he ain't a patch on the quiet Watson. There's a sleuth for you! Followed his man, he has, for months, I'll go bail; why, I'll bet he made his acquaintance at Ocean View just to keep right after him until he pulled something.

"And nobody suspected him all the while Sherlock was turning our little game into a damn nasty reality. I knew something was wrong—kind o' felt it, y'know—but it was too late to do anything when the suspicion grew to certainty. I was hobbled then.

"Oh, I give it to Holmes, fellows, he fooled me nicely! I came into my stateroom as we arranged, scattered those fool clues about, and was just ready to gather up the loot and blow off the gun out of the porthole, when in comes Sherlock like a ghost, slams me up against the wall and busts my nose, wraps me up in my own bathrobe and ties it with the cord, and carries me down below. Then he passed up again, and I heard the pistol go off, and there I've lain ever since until just now."

"By George! It was a clever bit of trickery," exclaimed a wide-eared listener. "Lucky it failed, eh?"

"Yes, thanks to Watson. I knew that chap was the real thing," vowed Percy, dabbing tenderly at his swollen nose. "You got to hand it to him, though he didn't deceive me for a minute. He had just the look of a real, clever crime-hound. I'll do something handsome for him when he comes on board."

None of the party wanted to go ashore until Watson had returned. They lounged under the awnings, sipping long cool drinks and chatting over the affair. About half an hour after Watson had taken his captive ashore, a wide-winged flying boat flew overhead close down, circled once or twice as if inspecting the fine yacht, then flew swiftly seaward in the general direction of a long line of islands belonging to many different nations, lying far down over the horizon. Flying boats have ceased to be objects of intense curiosity, and nobody took more than a fleeting interest in the low-flying machine, until it had almost speeded out of sight in the sea haze and the radio man suddenly appeared in obvious excitement and handed Percy a message. Percy read it idly, re-read it with staring eyes, dropped it on deck and sprang to the rail, gaping into the blue sky for that vanished speck which was the flying machine. The merry-eyed girl picked up the message, smoothed it out, and with a hesitating glance at the stupefied Percy read it aloud to the shocked company.

"Thank you, Percy," it said. "We've had a lovely time, and bear you no malice for your friends' ridicule of our methods. We'll write you from Mars, or Venus, or some place. Ta-ta, old boy. Sherlock and the Doctor."

Faces gaped into faces in utter amazement, then all turned to Percy. But Percy was already taking the companionway stairs six steps at a time, bound for his ravaged stateroom from which a treasure in gems and cash had all too surely vanished.

THE ADVENTURE OF THE DIAMOND NECKLACE

by G.F. Forrest

As I pushed open the door, I was greeted by the strains of a ravishing melody. Warlock Bones was playing dreamily on the accordion, and his keen, clear-cut face was almost hidden from view by the dense smoke-wreaths, which curled upwards from an exceedingly filthy briar-wood pipe. As soon as he saw me, he drew a final choking sob from the instrument, and rose to his feet with a smile of welcome.

"Ah, good morning, Goswell," he said cheerily. "But why do you press your trousers under the bed?"

It was true — quite true. This extraordinary observer, the terror of every cowering criminal, the greatest thinker that the world has ever known, had ruthlessly laid bare the secret of my life. Ah, it was true.

"But how did you know?" I asked in a stupor of amazement.

He smiled at my discomfiture.

"I have made a special study of trousers," he answered, "And of beds. I am rarely deceived. But, setting that knowledge, for the moment, on one side, have you forgotten the few days I spent with you three months ago? I saw you do it then."

He could never cease to astound me, this lynx-eyed sleuth of crime. I could never master the marvellous simplicity of his methods. I could only wonder and admire — a privilege, for which I can never be sufficiently grateful. I seated myself on the floor, and, embracing his left knee with both my arms in an ecstasy of passionate adoration, gazed up inquiringly into his intellectual countenance.

He rolled up his sleeve, and, exposing his thin nervous arm, injected half a pint of prussic acid with incredible rapidity. This operation finished, he glanced at the clock.

"In twenty-three or twenty-four minutes," he observed, "a man will probably call to see me. He has a wife, two children, and three false teeth, one of which will very shortly have to be renewed. He is a successful stockbroker of about forty-seven, wears Jaegers, and is an enthusiastic patron of Missing Word Competitions."

"How do you know all this?" I interrupted breathlessly, tapping his tibia with fond impatience.

Bones smiled his inscrutable smile.

"He will come," he continued, "to ask my advice about some jewels which were stolen from his house at Richmond last Thursday week. Among them was a diamond necklace of quite exceptional value."

"Explain," I cried in rapturous admiration. "Please explain."

"My dear Goswell," he laughed, "you are really very dense. Will you never learn my methods? The man is a personal friend of mine. I met him yesterday in the City, and he asked to come and talk over his loss with me this morning. *Voila tout.* Deduction, my good Goswell, mere deduction."

"But the jewels? Are the police on the track?"

"Very much off it. Really our police are the veriest bunglers. They have already arrested twenty-seven perfectly harmless and unoffending persons, including a dowager duchess, who is still prostrate with the shock; and, unless I am very much mistaken, they will arrest my friend's wife this afternoon. She was in Moscow at the time of the robbery, but that, of course, is of little consequence to these amiable dolts."

"And have you any clue as to the whereabouts of the jewels?"

"A fairly good one," he answered. "So good, in fact,

that I can at this present moment lay my hands upon them. It is a very simple case, one of the simplest I have ever had to deal with, and yet in its way a strange one, presenting several difficulties to the average observer. The motive of the robbery is a little puzzling. The thief appears to have been actuated not by the ordinary greed of gain so much as by an intense love of self-advertisement."

"I can hardly imagine," I said with some surprise, "a burglar, *qua* burglar, wishing to advertise his exploits to the world."

"True, Goswell. You show your usual common sense. But you have not the imagination, without which a detective can do nothing. Your position is that of those energetic, if somewhat beef-witted enthusiasts, the police. They are frankly puzzled by the whole affair. To me, personally, the case is as clear as daylight."

"That I can understand," I murmured with a reverent pat of his shin.

"The actual thief," he continued, "for various reasons I am unwilling to produce. But upon the jewels, as I said just now, I can lay my hand at any moment. Look here!"

He disentangled himself from my embrace, and walked to a patent safe in a corner of the room. From this he extracted a large jewel case, and, opening it, disclosed a set of the most superb diamonds. In the midst a magnificent necklace winked and flashed in the wintry sunlight. The sight took my breath away, and for a time I grovelled in speechless admiration before him.

"But — but how" — I stammered at last, and stopped, for he was regarding my confusion with evident amusement.

"I stole them," said Warlock Bones.

THE STOLEN CIGAR-CASE

by Bret Harte

I found Hemlock Jones in the old Brook Street lodgings, musing before the fire. With the freedom of an old friend I at once threw myself in my old familiar attitude at his feet, and gently caressed his boot. I was induced to do this for two reasons; one that it enabled me to get a good look at his bent, concentrated face, and the other that it seemed to indicate my reverence for his superhuman insight. So absorbed was he, even then, in tracking some mysterious clue, that he did not seem to notice me. But therein I was wrong — as I always was in my attempt to understand that powerful intellect.

"It is raining," he said, without lifting his head.

"You have been out then?" I said quickly.

"No. But I see that your umbrella is wet, and that your overcoat, which you threw off on entering, has drops of water on it."

I sat aghast at his penetration. After a pause he said carelessly, as if dismissing the subject: "Besides, I hear the rain on the window. Listen."

I listened. I could scarcely credit my ears, but there was the soft pattering of drops on the pane. It was evident, there was no deceiving this man!

"Have you been busy lately?" I asked, changing the subject. "What new problem — given up by Scotland Yard as inscrutable — has occupied that gigantic intellect?"

He drew back his foot slightly, and seemed to hesitate ere he returned it to its original position. Then he answered wearily: "Mere trifles — nothing to speak of. The Prince Kapoli has been here to get my advice regarding the disappearance of certain rubies from the Kremlin; the Rajah of

Pootibad, after vainly beheading his entire bodyguard, has been obliged to seek my assistance to recover a jewelled sword. The Grand Duchess of Pretzel-Brauntswig is desirous of discovering where her husband was on the night of the 14th of February, and last night" — he lowered his voice slightly — "a lodger in this very house, meeting me on the stairs, wanted to know 'Why they don't answer his bell.'"

I could not help smiling — until I saw a frown gathering on his inscrutable forehead.

"Pray to remember," he said coldly, "that it was through such an apparently trivial question that I found out, 'Why Paul Ferroll killed his Wife,' and 'What happened to Jones!'"

I became dumb at once. He paused for a moment, and then suddenly changing back to his usual pitiless, analytical style, he said: "When I say these are trifles — they are so in comparison to an affair that is now before me. A crime has been committed, and, singularly enough, against myself. You start," he said; "you wonder who would have dared attempt it! So did I; nevertheless, it has been done. *I* have been *robbed!*"

"*You* robbed — you, Hemlock Jones, the Terror of Peculators!" I gasped in amazement, rising and gripping the table as I faced him.

"Yes; listen. I would confess it to no other. But *you* who have followed my career, who know my methods; yea, for whom I have partly lifted the veil that conceals my plans from ordinary humanity; you, who have for years rapturously accepted my confidences, passionately admired my inductions and inferences, placed yourself at my beck and call, become my slave, grovelled at my feet, given up your practice except those few unremunerative and rapidly-decreasing patients to whom, in moments of abstraction over *my* problems, you have administered strychnine for quinine and arsenic for Epsom salts; you, who have sacrificed everything and everybody to me — *you* I make my confidant!"

I rose and embraced him warmly, yet he was already so engrossed in thought that at the same moment he mechanically placed his hand upon his watch chain as if to consult the time. "Sit down," he said; "have a cigar?"

"I have given up cigar smoking," I said.

"Why?" he asked.

I hesitated, and perhaps coloured. I had really given it up because, with my diminished practice, it was too expensive. I could only afford a pipe. "I prefer a pipe," I said laughingly. "But tell me of this robbery. What have you lost?"

He rose, and planting himself before the fire with his hands under his coat tails, looked down upon me reflectively for a moment. "Do you remember the cigar-case presented to me by the Turkish Ambassador for discovering the missing favourite of the Grand Vizier in the fifth chorus girl at the Hilarity Theatre? It was that one. It was incrusted with diamonds. I mean the cigar-case."

"And the largest one had been supplanted by paste," I said.

"Ah," he said with a reflective smile, "you know that?"

"You told me yourself. I remember considering it a proof of your extraordinary perception. But, by Jove, you don't mean to say you have lost it?"

He was silent for a moment. "No; it has been stolen, it is true, but I shall still find it. And by myself alone! In your profession, my dear fellow, when a member is severely ill he does not prescribe for himself, but call in a brother doctor. Therein we differ. I shall take this matter in my own hands."

"And where could you find better?" I said enthusiastically. "I should say the cigar-case is as good as recovered already."

"I shall remind you of that again," he said lightly. "And now, to show you my confidence in your judgment, in spite of my determination to pursue this alone, I am willing to listen to any suggestions from you."

He drew a memorandum book from his pocket, and, with a grave smile, took up his pencil.

I could scarcely believe my reason. He, the great Hemlock Jones! accepting suggestions from a humble individual like myself! I kissed his hand reverently, and began in a joyous tone:

"First I should advertise, offering a reward. I should give the same information in handbills, distributed at the 'pubs' and the pastry-cooks. I should next visit the different pawnbrokers; I should give notice at the police station. I should examine the servants. I should thoroughly search the house and my own pockets. I speak relatively," I added with a laugh, "of course I mean *your* own."

He gravely made an entry of these details.

"Perhaps," I added, "you have already done this?"

"Perhaps," he returned enigmatically. "Now, my dear friend," he continued, putting the notebook in his pocket, and rising — "would you excuse me for a few moments? Make yourself perfectly at home until I return; there may be some things," he added with a sweep of his hand towards his heterogeneously filled shelves, "that may interest you, and while away the time. There are pipes and tobacco in that corner and whiskey on the table." And nodding to me with the same inscrutable face, he left the room. I was too well accustomed to his methods to think much of his unceremonious withdrawal, and made no doubt he was off to investigate some clue which had suddenly occurred to his active intelligence.

Left to myself, I cast a cursory glance over his shelves. There were a number of small glass jars, containing earthy substances labeled "Pavement and road sweepings," from the principal thoroughfares and suburbs of London, with the sub-directions "For identifying foot tracks." There were several other jars labeled "Fluff from omnibus and road-car seats," "Cocoanut fibre and rope strands from mattings in public places," "Cigarette stumps and match ends from floor of Palace Theatre, Row A, 1 to 50." Everywhere were evidences of this wonderful man's system and perspicacity.

I was thus engaged when I heard the slight creaking of a door, and I looked up as a stranger entered. He was a rough-looking man, with a shabby overcoat, a still more disreputable muffler round his throat, and a cap on his head. Considerably annoyed at his intrusion I turned upon him rather sharply, when, with a mumbled, growling apology for mistaking the room, he shuffled out again and closed the door. I followed him quickly to the landing and saw that he disappeared down the stairs.

With my mind full of the robbery, the incident made a singular impression on me. I knew my friend's habits of hasty absences from his room in his moments of deep inspiration; it was only too probable that with his powerful intellect and magnificent perceptive genius concentrated on one subject, he should be careless of his own belongings, and, no doubt, even forget to take the ordinary precaution of locking up his drawers. I tried one or two and found I was right — although for some reason I was unable to open one to its fullest extent. The handles were sticky, as if someone had opened them with dirty fingers. Knowing Hemlock's fastidious cleanliness, I resolved to inform him of this circumstance, but I forgot it, alas! until — but I am anticipating my story.

His absence was strangely prolonged. I at last seated myself by the fire, and lulled by warmth and the patter of the rain on the window, I fell asleep. I may have dreamt, for during my sleep I had a vague semi-consciousness as of hands being softly pressed on my pockets — no doubt induced by the story of the robbery. When I came fully to my senses, I found Hemlock Jones sitting on the other side of the hearth, his deeply concentrated gaze fixed on the fire.

"I found you so comfortably asleep that I could not bear to waken you," he said with a smile.

I rubbed my eyes. "And what news?" I asked. "How have you succeeded?"

"Better than I expected," he said, "and I think," he added, tapping his note-book — "I owe much to *you*."

Deeply gratified, I awaited more. But in vain. I ought to have remembered that in his moods Hemlock Jones was reticence itself. I told him simply of the strange intrusion, but he only laughed.

Later, when I rose to go, he looked at me playfully. "If you were a married man," he said, "I would advise you not to go home until you had brushed your sleeve. There are a few short, brown seal-skin hairs on the inner side of the fore-arm — just where they would have adhered in your arm had encircled a seal-skin sacque with some pressure!"

"For once you are at fault," I said triumphantly, "the hair is my own as you will perceive; I had just had it cut at the hair-dressers, and no doubt this arm projected beyond the apron."

He frowned slightly, yet nevertheless, on my turning to go he embraced me warmly — a rare exhibition in that man of ice. He even helped me on with my overcoat and pulled out and smoothed down the flaps of my pockets. He was particular, too, in fitting my arm in my overcoat sleeve, shaking the sleeve down from the armhole to the cuff with his deft fingers. "Come again soon!" he said, clapping me on the back.

"At any and all times," I said enthusiastically. "I only ask ten minutes twice a day to eat a crust at my office and four hours sleep at night, and the rest of my time is devoted to you always — as you know."

"It is, indeed," he said, with his impenetrable smile.

Nevertheless I did not find him at home when I next called. One afternoon, when nearing my own home I met him in one of his favourite disguises — a long, blue, swallow-tailed coat, striped cotton trousers, large turn-over collar, blacked face, and white hat, carrying a tambourine. Of course to others the disguise was perfect, although it was known to myself, and I passed him — according to an old understanding between us — without the slightest recognition, trusting to a later explanation. At another time, as I was making a professional visit to the wife of a publican at the East End, I saw him in the disguise of a broken down artisan looking into the window of an adjacent pawnshop. I was delighted to see that he was evidently following my suggestions, and in my joy I ventured to tip him a wink; it was abstractedly returned.

Two days later I received a note appointing a meeting at his lodgings that night. That meeting, alas! was the one memorable occurrence of my life, and the last meeting I ever had with Hemlock Jones! I will try to set it down calmly, though my pulses still throb with the recollection of it.

I found him standing before the fire with that look upon his face which I had seen only once or twice in our acquaintance — a look which I may call an absolute concatenation of inductive and deductive ratiocination — from which all that was human, tender, or sympathetic, was absolutely discharged. He was simply an icy algebraic symbol! Indeed his whole being was concentrated to that extent that his clothes fitted loosely, and his head was absolutely so much reduced in size by his mental compression that his hat tipped back from his forehead and literally hung on his massive ears.

After I had entered, he locked the doors, fastened the windows, and even placed a chair before the chimney. As I watched those significant precautions with absorbing interest, he suddenly drew a revolver and presenting it to my temple, said in low, icy tones:

"Hand over that cigar-case!"

Even in my bewilderment, my reply was truthful, spontaneous, and involuntary. "I haven't got it," I said.

He smiled bitterly, and threw down his revolver. "I expected that reply! Then let me now confront you with something more awful, more deadly, more relentless and convincing than that mere lethal weapon — the damning inductive and deductive proofs of your guilt!" He drew from his pocket a roll of paper and a note-book.

"But surely," I gasped, "you are joking! You could not for a moment believe —"

"Silence!" he roared. "Sit down!"

I obeyed.

"You have condemned yourself," he went on pitilessly. "Condemned yourself on my processes — processes familiar to you, applauded by you, accepted by you for years! We will go back to the time when you first saw the cigar-case. Your expressions," he said in cold, deliberate tones, consulting his paper, "were: 'How beautiful! I wish it were mine.' This was your first step in crime — and my first indication. From 'I *wish* it were mine' to 'I *will* have it mine,' and the mere detail, 'How *can* I make it mine,' the advance was obvious. Silence! But as in my methods, it was necessary that there should be an overwhelming inducement to the crime, that unholy admiration of yours for the mere trinket itself was not enough. You are a smoker of cigars."

"But," I burst out passionately, "I told you I had given up smoking cigars."

"Fool!" he said coldly, "that is the *second* time you have committed yourself. Of course, you *told* me! what more natural than for you to blazon forth that prepared and unsolicited statement to *prevent* accusation. Yet, as I said before, even that wretched attempt to cover up your tracks was not enough. I still had to find that overwhelming, impelling motive necessary to affect a man like you. That motive I found in *passion*, the strongest of all impulses — love, I suppose you would call it," he added bitterly; "that night you called! You had brought the damning proofs of it in your sleeves."

"But," I almost screamed.

"Silence," he thundered, "I know what you would say. You would say that even if you had embraced some young person in a sealskin sacque what had that to do with the robbery. Let me tell you then, that that sealskin sacque represented the quality and character of your fatal entanglement! If you are at all conversant with light sporting literature you would know that a sealskin sacque indicates a love induced by sordid mercenary interests. You bartered your honour for it — that stolen cigar-case was the purchaser of the sealskin sacque! Without money, with a decreasing practice, it was the only way you could insure your passion being returned by that young person, whom, for your sake, I have not even pursued. Silence! Having thoroughly established your motive, I now proceed to the commission of the crime itself. Ordinary people would have begun with that — with an attempt to discover the whereabouts of the missing object. These are not my methods."

So overpowering was his penetration, that although I knew myself innocent, I licked my lips with avidity to hear the further details of this lucid exposition of my crime.

"You committed that theft the night I showed you the cigar-case and after I had carelessly thrown it in that drawer. You were sitting in that chair, and I had risen to take something from that shelf. In that instant you secured your booty without rising. Silence! Do you remember when I helped you on with your overcoat the other night? I was particular about fitting your arm in. While doing so I measured your arm with a spring tape measure from the shoulder to the cuff. A later visit to your tailor confirmed that measurement. It proved to be *the exact distance between your chair and that drawer!*"

I sat stunned.

"The rest are mere corroborative details! You were again tampering with the drawer when I discovered you doing so. Do not start! The stranger that blundered into the room with the muffler on — was myself. More, I had placed a little soap on the drawer handles when I purposely left you alone. The soap was on your hand when I shook it at parting. I softly felt your pockets when you were asleep for further developments. I embraced you when you left — that I might feel if you had the cigar-case, or any other articles, hidden on your body. This confirmed me in the belief that you had already disposed of it in the manner and for the purpose I have shown you. As I still believed you capable of remorse and confession, I allowed you to see I was on your track twice, once in the garb of an itinerant negro minstrel, and the second time as a workman looking in the window of the pawnshop where you pledged your booty."

"But," I burst out, "if you had asked the pawnbroker you would have seen how unjust —"

"Fool!" he hissed; "that was one of *your* suggestions to search the pawnshops. Do you suppose I followed any of your suggestions — the suggestions of the thief? On the contrary, they told me what to avoid."

"And I suppose," I said bitterly, "you have not even searched your drawer."

"No," he said calmly.

I was for the first time really vexed. I went to the nearest drawer and pulled it out sharply. It stuck as it had before, leaving a part of the drawer unopened. By working it, however, I discovered that it was impeded by some obstacle that had slipped to the upper part of the drawer, and held it firmly fast. Inserting my hand, I pulled out the impeding object. It was the missing cigar-case. I turned to him with a cry of joy.

But I was appalled at his expression. A look of contempt was now added to his acute, penetrating gaze. "I have been mistaken," he said slowly. "I had not allowed for your weakness and cowardice. I thought too highly of you even in your guilt; but I see now why you tampered with that drawer the other night. By some incredible means — possibly another theft — you took the cigar-case out of pawn, and like a whipped hound restored it to me in this feeble, clumsy fashion. You thought to deceive me, Hemlock Jones: more, you thought to destroy my infallibility. Go! I give you your liberty. I shall not summon the three policemen who wait in the adjoining room — but out of my sight for ever."

As I stood once more dazed and petrified, he took me firmly by the ear and led me into the hall, closing the door behind him. This re-opened presently wide enough to permit him to thrust out my hat, overcoat, umbrella and overshoes, and then closed against me for ever!

I never saw him again. I am bound to say, however, that thereafter my business increased — I recovered much of my old practice — and a few of my patients recovered also. I became rich. I had a brougham and a house in the West End. But I often wondered, pondering on that wonderful man's penetration and insight, if, in some lapse of consciousness, I had not really stolen his cigar-case!

THE ADVENTURES OF SHAMROCK JOLNES

by O. Henry

I am so fortunate as to count Shamrock Jolnes, the great New York detective, among my muster of friends. Jolnes is what is called the "inside man" of the city detective force. He is an expert in the use of the typewriter, and it is his duty, whenever there is a "murder mystery" to be solved, to sit at a desk telephone at headquarters and take down the message of "cranks" who 'phone in their confessions to having committed the crime.

But on certain "off" days when confessions are coming in slowly and three or four newspapers have run to earth as many different guilty persons, Jolnes will knock about the town with me, exhibiting, to my great delight and instruction, his marvellous powers of observation and deduction.

The other day I dropped in at Headquarters and found the great detective gazing thoughtfully at a string that was tied tightly around his tattle finger.

"Good morning, Whatsup," he said, without turning his head. "I'm glad to notice that you've had your house fitted up with electric lights at last."

"Will you please tell me," I said, in surprise, "how you knew that? I am sure that I never mentioned the fact to any one, and the wiring was a rush order not completed until this morning."

"Nothing easier," said Jolnes, genially. "As you came in I caught the odor of the cigar you are smoking. I know an expensive cigar; and I know that not more than three men in New York can afford to smoke cigars and pay gas bills too at the present time. That was an easy one. But I am working just now on a little problem of my own."

"Why have you that string on your finger?" I asked.

"That's the problem," said Jolnes. "My wife tied that on this morning to remind me of something I was to send up to the house. Sit down, Whatsup, and excuse me for a few moments."

The distinguished detective went to a wall telephone, and stood with the receiver to his ear for probably ten minutes.

"Were you listening to a confession?" I asked, when he had returned to his chair.

"Perhaps," said Jolnes, with a smile, "it might be called something of the sort. To be frank with you, Whatsup, I've cut out the dope. I've been increasing the quantity for so long that morphine doesn't have much effect on me any more. I've got to have something more powerful. That telephone I just went to is connected with a room in the Waldorf where there's an author's reading in progress. Now, to get at the solution of this string."

After five minutes of silent pondering, Jolnes looked at me, with a smile, and nodded his head.

"Wonderful man!" I exclaimed; "already?"

"It is quite simple," he said, holding up his finger. "You see that knot? That is to prevent my forgetting. It is, therefore, a forget-me-knot. A forget-me-not is a flower. It was a sack of flour that I was to send home!"

"Beautiful!" I could not help crying out in admiration.

"Suppose we go out for a ramble," suggested Jolnes.

"There is only one case of importance on hand now. Old man McCarty, one hundred and four years old, died from eating too many bananas. The evidence points so strongly to the Mafia that the police have surrounded the Second Avenue Katzenjammer Gambrinus Club No. 2, and the capture of the assassin is only the matter of a few hours. The detective force has not yet been called on for assistance."

Jolnes and I went out and up the street toward the

corner, where we were to catch a surface car.

Halfway up the block we met Rheingelder, an acquaintance of ours, who held a City Hall position.

"Good morning, Rheingelder," said Jolnes, halting. "Nice breakfast that was you had this morning."

Always on the lookout for the detective's remarkable feats of deduction, I saw Jolnes's eyes flash for an instant upon a long yellow splash on the shirt bosom and a smaller one upon the chin of Rheingelder — both undoubtedly made by the yolk of an egg.

"Oh, dot is some of your defectiveness," said Rheingelder, shaking all over with a smile. "Vell, I bet you trinks and cigars all around dot you cannot tell vot I haf eaten for breakfast."

"Done," said Jolnes. "Sausage, pumpernickel, and coffee."

Rheingelder admitted the correctness of the surmise and paid the bet. When we had proceeded on our way I said to Jolnes:

"I thought you looked at the egg spilled on his chin and shirt front."

"I did," said Jolnes. "That is where I began my deduction. Rheingelder is a very economical, saving man. Yesterday eggs dropped in the market to twenty-eight cents per dozen. Today they are quoted a forty-two. Rheingelder ate eggs yesterday, and to-day he went back to his usual fare. A little thing like this isn't anything, Whatsup; it belongs to the primary arithmetic class."

When we boarded the street car we found the seats all occupied — principally by ladies. Jolnes and I stood on the rear platform.

About the middle of the car there sat an elderly man with a short, gray beard, who looked to be the typical, well-dressed New Yorker. At successive corners other ladies climbed aboard, and soon three or four of them were standing over the man, clinging to straps and glaring meaningly at the man who occupied the coveted seat. But he resolutely retained his place.

"We New Yorkers," I remarked to Jolnes, "have about lost our manners, as far as the exercise of them in public goes."

"Perhaps so," said Jolnes, lightly; "but the man you evidently refer to happens to be a very chivalrous and courteous gentleman from Old Virginia. He is spending a few days in New York with his wife and two daughters, and he leaves for the South to-night."

"You know him, then?" I said, in amazement.

"I never saw him before we stepped on the car," declared the detective, smilingly.

"By the gold tooth of the Witch of Endor!" I cried, "if you can construe all at from his appearance you are dealing in nothing else than black art."

"The habit of observation — nothing more," said Jolnes. "If the old gentleman gets off the car before we do, I think I can demonstrate to you the accuracy of my deduction."

Three blocks farther along the gentleman rose to leave the car. Jolnes addressed him at the door:

"Pardon me, sir, but are you not Colonel Hunter, of Norfolk, Virginia?"

"No, suh," was the extremely courteous answer. "My name, suh, is Ellison — Major Cornfield R. Ellison, from Fairfax County, in the same state. I know a good many people, suh, in Norfolk — the Goodriches, the Tollivers, and the Crabtrees, suh, but I never had the pleasure of meeting yo' friend, Colonel Hunter. I am happy to say, suh, that I am going back to Virginia to-night, after having spent a week in yo' city with my wife and three daughters. I shall be in Norfolk in about ten days, and if you will give me yo name, suh, I will take pleasure in looking up Colonel Hunter and telling him that you inquired after him, suh."

"Thank you," said Jolnes; "tell him that Reynolds sent his regards, if you will be so kind."

I glanced at the great New York detective and saw that a look of intense chagrin had come upon his clear-cut features. Failure in the slightest point always galled Shamrock Jolnes.

"Did you say your *three* daughters?" he asked of the Virginia gentleman.

"Yes, suh, my three daughters, all as fine girls as there are in Fairfax County," was the answer.

With that Major Ellison stopped the car and began to descend the step.

Shamrock Jolnes clutched his arm.

"One moment, sir," he begged, in an urbane voice in which I alone detected the anxiety — "am I not right in believing that one of the young ladies is an *adopted* daughter?"

"You are, suh," admitted the major, from the ground, "but how the devil you knew it, suh, is mo' than I can tell."

"And mo' than I can tell, too," I said, as the car went on.

Jolnes was restored to his calm, observant serenity by having wrested victory from his apparent failure; so after we got off the car he invited me into a cafe promising to reveal the process of his latest wonderful feat.

"In the first place," he began after we were comfortably seated, "I knew the gentleman was no New Yorker because he was flushed and uneasy and restless on account of the ladies that were standing, although he did not rise and give them his seat. I decided from his appearance that he was a Southerner rather than a Westerner.

"Next I began to figure out his reason for not relinquishing his seat to a lady when he evidently felt strongly, but not overpoweringly, impelled to do so. I very quickly decided upon that. I noticed that one of his eyes had received a severe jab in one corner, which was red and inflamed, and that all over his face were tiny round marks about the size of the end of an uncut lead pencil. Also upon both of his patent-leather shoes were a number of deep imprints shaped like ovals cut off square at one end.

"Now, there is only one district in New York City where a man is bound to receive scars and wounds and indentations of that sort — and that is along the sidewalks of Twenty-third Street and a portion of Sixth Avenue south of there. I knew from the imprints of tramp-ring French heels on his feet and the marks of countless jabs in the face from umbrellas and parasols carried by women in the shopping district that he had been in conflict with the amazonian troops. And as he was a man of intelligent appearance, I knew he would not have braved such dangers unless he had been dragged thither by his own women folk. Therefore, when he got on the car his anger at the treatment he had received was sufficient to make him keep his seat in spite of his traditions of Southern chivalry."

"That is all very well," I said, "but why did you insist upon daughters — and especially two daughters? Why couldn't a wife alone have taken him shopping?"

"There had to be daughters," said Jolnes, calmly. "If he had only a wife, and she near his own age, he could have bluffed her into going alone. If he had a young wife she would prefer to go alone. So there you are."

"I'll admit that," I said; "but, now, why two daughters? And how; in the name of all the prophets, did you guess that one was adopted when he told you he had three?"

"Don't say guess," said Jolnes, with a touch of pride in his air; "there is no such word in the lexicon of ratiocination. In Major Ellison's buttonhole there was a carnation and a rosebud backed by a geranium leaf. No woman ever combined a carnation and a rosebud into a boutonnière. Close your eyes, Whatsup, and give the logic of your imagination a chance. Can not you see the lovely Adele fastening the carnation to the lapel so that papa may be gay upon the street? And then the romping Edith May dancing up with sisterly jealousy to add her rosebud to the adornment?"

"And then," I cried, beginning to feel enthusiasm, "when he declared that he had three daughters —"

"I could see," said Jolnes, "one in the background who added no flower; and I knew that she must be —"

"Adopted!" I broke in. "I give you every credit; but how did you know he was leaving for the South to-night?"

"In his breast pocket," said the great detective, "something large and oval made a protuberance. Good liquor is scarce on trains, and it is a long journey from New York to Fairfax County."

"Again, I must bow to you," I said. "And tell me this, so that my last shred of doubt will be cleared away; why did you decide that he was from Virginia?"

"It was very faint, I admit," answered Shamrock Jolnes, "but no trained observer could have failed to detect the odor of mint in the car."

MR. RAFFLES HOLMES

by John Kendrick Bangs

I

INTRODUCING MR. RAFFLES HOLMES

It was a blistering night in August. All day long the mercury in the thermometer had been flirting with the figures at the top of the tube, and the promised shower at night which a mendacious Weather Bureau had been prophesying as a slight mitigation of our sufferings was conspicuous wholly by its absence. I had but one comfort in the sweltering hours of the day, afternoon and evening, and that was that my family were away in the mountains, and there was no law against my sitting around all day clad only in my pajamas, and otherwise concealed from possibly intruding eyes by the wreaths of smoke that I extracted from the nineteen or twenty cigars which, when there is no protesting eye to suggest otherwise, form my daily allowance. I had tried every method known to the resourceful flat-dweller of modern times to get cool and to stay so, but alas, it was impossible. Even the radiators, which all winter long had never once given forth a spark of heat, now hissed to the touch of my moistened finger. Enough cooling drinks to float an ocean greyhound had passed into my inner man, with no other result than to make me perspire more profusely than ever, and in so far as sensations went, to make me feel hotter than before.

Finally, as a last resource, along about midnight, its gridiron floor having had a chance to lose some of its stored-up warmth, I climbed out upon the fire-escape at the rear of the Richmere, hitched my hammock from one of the railings thereof to the leader running from the roof to the area, and swung myself therein some eighty feet above the concealed pavement of our backyard — so called, perhaps, because of its dimensions which were just about that square.

It was a little improvement, though nothing to brag of. What fitful zephyrs there might be, caused no doubt by the rapid passage to and fro on the roof above and fence-tops below of vagrant felines on Cupid's contentious battles bent, to the disturbance of the still air, soughed softly through the meshes of my hammock and gave some measure of relief, grateful enough for which I ceased the perfervid language I had been using practically since sunrise, and dozed off. And then there entered upon the scene that marvelous man, Raffles Holmes, of whose exploits it is the purpose of these papers to tell.

I had dozed perhaps for a full hour when the first strange sounds grated upon my ear. Somebody had opened a window in the kitchen of the first-floor apartment below, and with a dark lantern was inspecting the iron platform of the fire escape without. A moment later this somebody crawled out of the window, and with movements that in themselves were a sufficient indication of the questionable character of his proceedings, made for the ladder leading to the floor above, upon which many a time and oft had I too climbed to home and safety when an inconsiderate janitor had locked me out. Every step that he took was stealthy — that much I could see by the dim starlight. His lantern he had turned dark again, evidently lest he should attract attention in the apartments below as he passed their windows in his upward flight.

"Ha! ha!" thought I to myself. "It's never too hot for Mr. Sneak to get in his fine work. I wonder whose stuff he is after?"

Turning over flat on my stomach so that I might the more readily observe the man's movements, and breathing *pianissimo* lest he in turn should observe mine, I watched him as he climbed. Up he came as silently as the midnight mouse upon a soft carpet — up past the Jorkins' apartments on the second floor; up stealthily by the Tinkletons' abode on the third; up past the fire escape Italian garden of little Mrs. Persimmon on the fourth; up past the windows of the disagreeable Garraways' kitchen below mine, and then, with the easy grace of a feline, zip! he silently landed within reach of my hand on my own little iron veranda, and craning his neck to one side peered in through the open window and listened intently for two full minutes.

"Humph!" whispered my inner consciousness to itself. "He is the coolest thing I've seen since last Christmas left town. I wonder what he is up to? There's nothing in my apartment worth stealing, now that my wife and children are away, unless it be my Jap valet, Nogi, who might make a very excellent cab driver if I could only find words to convey to his mind the idea that he is discharged."

And then the visitor, apparently having correctly assured himself that there was no one within, stepped across the window sill and vanished into the darkness of my kitchen. A moment later I too entered the window in pursuit — not so close a one, however, as to acquaint him with my proximity. I wanted to see what the chap was up to; and also being totally unarmed and ignorant as to whether or not he carried dangerous weapons, I determined to go slow for a little while. Moreover, the situation was not wholly devoid of novelty, and it seemed to me that here at last was abundant opportunity for a new sensation.

As he had entered, so did he walk cautiously along the narrow bowling alley that serves for a hallway connecting my drawing room and library with the dining room, until he came to the library, into which he disappeared. This was not reassuring to me, because, to tell the truth, I value my books more than I do my plate, and if I were to be robbed I should much have preferred his taking my plated plate from the dining room than any one of my editions-deluxe sets of the works of Marie Corelli, Hall Caine, and other standard authors from the library shelves.

Once in the library, he quietly drew the shades at the windows thereof to bar possible intruding eyes from without, turned on the electric lights, and proceeded to go through my papers as calmly and coolly as though they were his own. In a short time, apparently, he found what he wanted in the shape of a royalty statement recently received by me from my publishers, and, lighting one of my cigars from a bundle of brevas in front of him, took off his coat and sat down to peruse the statement of my returns.

Simple though it was, this act aroused the first feeling of resentment in my breast, for the relations between the author and his publishers are among the most sacred confidences of life, and the peeping Tom who peers through a keyhole at the courtship of a young man engaged in wooing his *fiancée* is no worse an intruder than he who would tear aside the veil of secrecy which screens the official returns of a "best seller" from the public eye.

Feeling, therefore, that I had permitted matters to proceed as far as they might with propriety, I instantly entered the room and confronted my uninvited guest, bracing myself, of course, for the defensive onslaught which I naturally expected to sustain. But nothing of the sort occurred, for the intruder, with a composure that was nothing short of marvelous under the circumstances, instead of rising hurriedly like one caught in some disreputable act, merely leaned farther back in the chair, took the cigar from his mouth, and greeted me with:

"Howdy do, sir. What can I do for you this beastly hot night?"

The cold rim of a revolver-barrel placed at my temple could not more effectually have put me out of business than this nonchalant reception. Consequently I gasped out something about its being the sultriest 47th of August in eighteen years, and plumped back into a chair opposite him.

"I wouldn't mind a Remsen cooler myself," he went on, "but the fact is your butler is off for tonight, and I'm hanged if I can find a lemon in the house. Maybe you'll join me in a smoke?" he added, shoving my own bundle of brevas across the table. "Help yourself."

"I guess I know where the lemons are," said I. "But how did you know my butler was out?"

"I telephoned him to go to Philadelphia this afternoon to see his brother Yoku, who is ill there," said my visitor. "You see, I didn't want him around tonight when I called. I knew I could manage you alone in case you turned up, as you see you have, but two of you, and one a Jap, I was afraid might involve us all in ugly complications. Between you and me, Jenkins, these Orientals are pretty lively fighters, and your man Nogi particularly has got jiu-jitsu down to a pretty fine point, so I had to do something to get rid of him. Our arrangement is a matter for two, not three, anyhow."

"So," said I, coldly. "You and I have an arrangement, have we? I wasn't aware of it."

"Not yet," he answered. "But there's a chance that we may have. If I can only satisfy myself that you are the man I'm looking for, there is no earthly reason that I can see why we should not come to terms. Go on out and get the lemons and the gin and soda, and let's talk this thing over man to man like a couple of good fellows at the club. I mean you no harm, and you certainly don't wish to do any kind of injury to a chap who, even though appearances are against him, really means to do you a good turn."

"Appearances certainly are against you, sir," said I, a trifle warmly, for the man's composure was irritating. "A disappearance would be more likely to do you credit at this moment,"

"Tush, Jenkins!" he answered. "Why waste breath say-ing self-evident things? Here you are on the verge of a big transaction, and you delay proceedings by making statements of fact, mixed in with a cheap wit which, I must confess, I find surprising, and so obvious as to be visible even to the blind. You don't talk like an author whose stuff is worth ten cents a word — more like a penny-a-liner, in fact, with whom words are of such small value that no one's the loser if he throws away a whole dictionary. Go out and mix a couple of your best Remsen coolers, and by the time you get back I'll have got to the gist of this royalty statement of yours, which is all I've come for. Your silver and books and love letters and manuscripts are safe from me. I wouldn't have 'em as a gift."

"What concern have you with my royalties?" I demanded.

"A vital one," said he. "Mix the coolers, and when you get back I'll tell you. Go on. There's a good chap. It'll be daylight before long, and I want to close up this job if I can before sunrise."

What there was in the man's manner to persuade me to compliance with his wishes, I am sure I cannot say definitely. There was a cold, steely glitter in his eye, for one thing. With it, however, was a strengthfulness of purpose, a certain pleasant masterfulness, that made me feel that I could trust him, and it was to this aspect of his nature that I yielded. There was something frankly appealing in his long, thin, ascetic looking face, and I found it irresistible.

"All right," said I with a smile and a frown to express the conflicting quality of my emotions. "So be it. I'll get the coolers, but you must remember, my friend, that there are coolers and coolers, just as there are jugs and jugs. The kind of jug that remains for you will depend upon the story you have to tell when I get back, so you'd better see that it's a good one."

"I am not afraid, Jenkins, old chap," he said with a

hearty laugh as I rose. "If this royalty statement can prove to me that you are the literary partner I need in my business, I can prove to you that I'm a good man to tie up to — so go along with you."

With this he lighted a fresh cigar and turned to a perusal of my statement, which, I am glad to say, was a good one, owing to the great success of my book, *Wild Animals I Have Never Met* — the seventh-best seller at Rochester, Watertown, and Miami in June and July, 1905.

I went out into the dining room and mixed the coolers. As you may imagine, I was not long at it, for my curiosity over my visitor lent wings to my corkscrew, and in five minutes I was back with the tempting beverages in the tall glasses, the lemon curl giving it the vertebrate appearance that all stiff drinks should have, and the ice tinkling refreshingly upon the sultry air.

"There," said I, placing his glass before him. "Drink hearty, and then to business. Who are you?"

"There is my card," he replied, swallowing a goodly half of the cooler and smacking his lips appreciatively, and tossing a visiting card across to me on the other side of the table. I picked up the card and read as follows: "Mr. Raffles Holmes, London and New York."

"Raffles Holmes?" I cried in amazement.

"The same, Mr. Jenkins," said he. "I am the son of Sherlock Holmes, the famous detective, and grandson of A. J. Raffles, the distinguished — er — ah — cricketer, sir."

I gazed at him, dumb with astonishment.

"You've heard of my father, Sherlock Holmes?" asked my visitor.

I confessed that the name of the gentleman was not unfamiliar to me.

"And Mr. Raffles, my grandfather?" he persisted.

"If there ever was a story of that fascinating man that I have not read, Mr. Holmes," said I, "I beg you will let me have it."

"Well, then," said he with that quick, nervous manner which proved him a true son of Sherlock Holmes, "did it never occur to you as an extraordinary happening, as you read of my father's wonderful powers as a detective, and of Raffles' equally wonderful prowess as a — er — well, let us not mince words — as a thief, Mr. Jenkins, the two men operating in England at the same time, that no story ever appeared in which Sherlock Holmes's genius was pitted against the subtly planned misdeeds of Mr. Raffles? Is it not surprising that with two such men as they were, working out their destinies in almost identical grooves of daily action, they should never have crossed each other's paths as far as the public is the wiser, and in the very nature of the conflicting interests of their respective lines of action as foemen, the one pursuing, the other pursued, they should to the public's knowledge never have clashed?"

"Now that you speak of it," said I, "it was rather extraordinary that nothing of the sort happened. One would think that the sufferers from the depredations of Raffles would immediately have gone to Holmes for assistance in bringing the other to justice. Truly, as you intimate, it was strange that they never did."

"Pardon me, Jealous," put in my visitor. "I never intimated anything of the sort. What I intimated was that no story of any such conflict ever came to light. As a matter of fact, Sherlock Holmes was put upon a Raffles case in 1883, and while success attended upon every step of it, and my grandfather was run to earth by him as easily as was ever any other criminal in Holmes's grip, a little naked god called Cupid stepped in, saved Raffles from jail, and wrote the word failure across Holmes's docket of the case. *I, sir, am the only tangible result of Lord Dorrington's retainers to Sherlock Holmes.*"

"You speak enigmatically, after the occasional fashion

of your illustrious father," said I. "The Dorrington case is unfamiliar to me,"

"Naturally so," said my *vis-à-vis*. "Because, save to my father, my grandfather, and myself, the details are unknown to anybody. Not even my mother knew of the incident, and as for Dr. Watson and Bunny, the scribes through whose industry the adventures of those two great men were respectively narrated to an absorbed world, they didn't even know there had ever been a Dorrington case, because Sherlock Holmes never told Watson and Raffles never told Bunny. But they both told me, and now that I am satisfied that there is a demand for your books, I am willing to tell it to you with the understanding that we share and share alike in the profits if perchance you think well enough of it to write it up."

"Go on!" I said. "I'll whack up with you square and honest."

"Which is more than either Watson or Bunny ever did with my father or my grandfather, else I should not be in the business which now occupies my time and attention," said Raffles Holmes with a cold snap to his eyes which I took as an admonition to hew strictly to the line of honor, or to subject myself to terrible consequences. "With that understanding, Jenkins, I'll tell you the story of the Dorrington Ruby Seal, in which some crime, a good deal of romance, and my ancestry are involved."

II
THE ADVENTURE OF
THE DORRINGTON RUBY SEAL

"Lord Dorrington, as you may have heard," said Raffles Holmes, leaning back in my easychair and gazing reflectively up at the ceiling, "was chiefly famous in England as a sporting peer. His vast estates, in five counties, were always open to any sportsman of renown, or otherwise, as long as he was a true sportsman. So open, indeed, was the house that he kept that, whether he was there or not, little weekend parties of members of the sporting fraternity used to be got up at a moment's notice to run down to Dorrington Castle, Devonshire; to Dorrington Lodge on the Isle of Wight; to Dorrington Hall, near Dublin, or to any of his other country places for over Sunday.

"Sometimes there'd be a lot of turf people; sometimes a dozen or more devotees of the prize-ring; not infrequently a gathering of the best known cricketers of the time, among whom, of course, my grandfather, A. J. Raffles, was conspicuous. For the most part, the cricketers never partook of Dorrington's hospitality save when his lordship was present, for your cricket-player is a bit more punctilious in such matters than your turfmen or ring-side habitués. It so happened one year, however, that his lordship was absent from England for the better part of eight months, and, when the time came for the annual cricket gathering at his Devonshire place, he cabled his London representative to see to it that everything was carried on just as if he were present, and that everyone should be invited for the usual week's play and pleasure at Dorrington Castle. His instructions were carried out to the letter and, save for the fact that the genial host was absent, the house-party went through to perfection. My grandfather, as usual, was the life of the occasion, and all went merry as a marriage bell. Seven months later, Lord Dorrington returned, and, a week after that, the loss of the Dorrington jewels from the Devonshire strong-boxes was a matter of common knowledge. When, or by whom, they had been taken was an absolute mystery. As far as anybody could find out, they might have been taken the night before his return, or the night after his departure. The only fact in sight was that they were gone — Lady Dorrington's diamonds, a half dozen valuable jeweled rings belonging to his lordship, and, most irremediable of losses, the famous ruby seal which George IV had given to Dorrington's grandfather, Sir Arthur Deering, as a token of his personal esteem during the period of the Regency. This was a flawless ruby, valued at some six or seven thousand pounds sterling, in which had been cut the Deering arms surrounded by a garter upon which were engraved the words, 'Deering Ton,' which the family, upon Sir Arthur's elevation to the peerage in 1836, took as its title, or Dorrington. His lordship was almost prostrated by the loss. The diamonds and the rings, although valued at thirty thousand pounds, he could easily replace, but the personal associations of the seal were such that nothing, no amount of money, could duplicate the lost ruby."

"So that his first act," I broke in, breathlessly, "was to send for —"

"Sherlock Holmes, my father," said Raffles Holmes. "Yes, Mr. Jenkins, the first thing Lord Dorrington did was to telegraph to London for Sherlock Holmes, requesting him to come immediately to Dorrington Castle and assume charge of the case. Needless to say, Mr. Holmes dropped everything else and came. He inspected the gardens, measured the road from the railway station to the castle, questioned all the servants; was particularly insistent upon knowing where the parlor-maid was on the 13th of January; secured accurate information as to the personal habits of his lordship's dachshund Nicholas; subjected the chef to a cross-examination that covered every point of his life, from his remote ancestry to his receipt for baking apples; gathered up three suitcases of sweepings from his lordship's private apartment, and two boxes containing three each of every variety of cigars that Lord Dorrington had laid down in his cellar. As you are aware, Sherlock Holmes, in his prime, was a great master of detail. He then departed for London, taking with him an impression in wax of the missing seal, which Lord Dorrington happened to have preserved in his escritoire.

"On his return to London, Holmes inspected the seal carefully under a magnifying glass, and was instantly impressed with the fact that it was not unfamiliar to him. He had seen it somewhere before, but where? That was now the question uppermost in his mind. Prior to this, he had never had any communication with Lord Dorrington, so that, if it was in his correspondence that the seal had formerly come to him, most assuredly the person who had used it had come by it dishonestly. Fortunately, at that time, it was a habit of my father's never to destroy papers of any sort. Every letter that he ever received was classified and filed, envelope and all. The thing to do, then, was manifestly to run over the files and find the letter, if indeed it was in or on a letter that the seal had first come to his attention. It was a herculean job, but that never fazed Sherlock Holmes, and he went at it tooth and nail. Finally his effort was rewarded. Under 'Applications for Autograph' he found a daintily scented little missive from a young girl living at Goring-Streatley on the Thames, the daughter, she said, of a retired missionary — the Reverend James Tattersby — asking him if he would not kindly write his autograph upon the enclosed slip for her collection. It was the regular stock application that truly distinguished men receive in every mail. The only thing to distinguish it from other applications was the beauty of the seal on the fly of the envelope, which attracted his passing notice and was then filed away with the other letters of similar import.

"'Ho! ho!' quoth Holmes, as he compared the two impressions and discovered that they were identical. 'An innocent little maiden who collects autographs, and a retired missionary in possession of the Dorrington seal, eh? Well, that *is* interesting. I think I shall run down to Goring-Streatley over Sunday and meet Miss Marjorie Tattersby and her reverend father. I'd like to see to what style of people I have intrusted my autograph.'

"To decide was to act with Sherlock Holmes, and the following Saturday, hiring a canoe at Windsor, he made his way up the river until he came to the pretty little hamlet, snuggling in the Thames Valley, if such it may be called, where the young lady and her good father were dwelling. Fortune favored him in that his prey was still there — both much respected by the whole community; the father a fine looking, really splendid specimen of a man whose presence alone carried a conviction of integrity and lofty mind; the daughter — well, to see her was to love her, and the moment the eyes of Sherlock fell upon her face, that great heart of his, that had ever been adamant to beauty, a very Gibraltar against the wiles of the other sex, went down in the chaos of a first and overwhelming passion. So hard hit was he by Miss Tattersby's beauty that his chief thought now was to avert rather than to direct suspicion towards her. After all, she might have come into possession of the jewel honestly, though how the daughter of a retired missionary, considering its intrinsic value, could manage such a thing, was pretty hard to understand, and he fled back to London to think it over. Arrived there, he found an invitation to visit Dorrington Castle again *incog.* Lord Dorrington was to have a mixed weekend party over the following Sunday, and this, he thought, would give Holmes an opportunity to observe the characteristics of Dorrington's visitors and possibly gain some clue as to the light-fingered person from whose depredations his lordship had suffered. The idea commended itself to Holmes, and in the disguise of a young American clergyman, whom Dorrington had met in the States, the following Friday found him at Dorrington Castle.

"Well, to make a long story short," said Raffles Holmes, "the young clergyman was introduced to many of the leading sportsmen of the hour, and, for the most part, they passed muster, but one of them did not, and that was the well known cricketer A. J. Raffles, for the moment Raffles entered the room, jovially greeting everybody about him, and was presented to Lord Dorrington's new guest, Sherlock Holmes recognized in him no less a person than the Reverend James Tattersby, retired missionary of Goring-Streatley-on-Thames, and the father of the woman who had filled his soul with love and yearning of the truest sort. The problem was solved. Raffles was, to all intents and purposes, caught with the goods on. Holmes could have exposed him then and there had he chosen to do so, but every time it came to the point the lovely face of Marjorie Tattersby came between him and his purpose. How could he inflict the pain and shame which the exposure of her father's misconduct would certainly entail upon that fair woman, whose beauty and fresh innocence had taken so strong a hold upon his heart? No — that was out of the question. The thing to do, clearly, was to visit Miss Tattersby during her father's absence and, if possible, ascertain from her just how she had come into possession of the seal, before taking further steps in the matter. This he did. Making sure, to begin with, that Raffles was to remain at Dorrington Hall for the coming ten days, Holmes had himself telegraphed for and returned to London. There he wrote himself a letter of introduction to the Reverend James Tattersby, on the paper of the Anglo-American Missionary Society, a sheet of which he secured in the public writing-room of that institution, armed with which he returned to the beautiful little spot on the Thames where the Tattersbys abode. He spent the night at the inn, and, in conversation with the landlord and boatmen, learned much that was interesting concerning the Reverend James. Among other things, he discovered that this gentleman and his daughter had been respected residents of the place for three years; that Tattersby was rarely seen in the daytime about the place; that he was unusually fond of canoeing at night, which, he said, gave him the quiet and solitude necessary for that reflection which is so essential to the spiritual being of a minister of grace; that he frequently indulged in long absences, during which time it was supposed that he was engaged in the work of his calling. He appeared to be a man of some, but not of lavish, means. The most notable and suggestive thing, however, that Holmes ascertained in his conversation with the boatmen was that, at the time of the famous Cliveden robbery, when several thousand pounds' worth of plate had been taken from the great hall, that later fell into the possession of a well known American hotel-keeper, Tattersby, who happened to be on the river late that night, was, according to his own statement, the unconscious witness of the escape of the thieves on board a mysterious steam-launch, which the police were never able afterwards to locate. They had nearly upset his canoe with the wash of their rapidly moving craft as they sped past him after having stowed their loot safely on board. Tattersby had supposed them to be employees of the estate and never gave the matter another thought until three days later, when the news of the robbery was published to the world. He had immediately communicated the news of what he had seen to the police, and had done all that lay in his power to aid them in locating the robbers, but all to no purpose. From that day to this the mystery of the Cliveden plot had never been solved.

"The following day Holmes called at the Tattersby cottage, and was fortunate enough to find Miss Tattersby at home. His previous impression as to her marvelous beauty was more than confirmed, and each moment that he talked to her she revealed new graces of manner that completed the capture of his hitherto unsusceptible heart. Miss Tattersby regretted her father's absence. He had gone, she said, to attend a secret missionary conference at Pentwllycod in

Wales and was not expected back for a week, all of which quite suited Sherlock Holmes. Convinced that, after years of waiting, his affinity had at last crossed his path, he was in no hurry for the return of that parent, who would put an instant quietus upon this affair of the heart. Manifestly the thing for him to do was to win the daughter's hand and then intercept the father, acquaint him with his aspirations, and compel acquiescence by the force of his knowledge of Raffles's misdeed. Hence, instead of taking his departure immediately, he remained at the Goring-Streatley Inn, taking care each day to encounter Miss Tattersby on one pretext or another, hoping that their acquaintance would ripen into friendship, and then into something warmer. Nor was the hope a vain one, for when the fair Marjorie learned that it was the visitor's intention to remain in the neighborhood until her father's return, she herself bade him to make use of the old gentleman's library, to regard himself always as a welcome daytime guest. She even suggested pleasant walks through the neighboring country and little canoe trips up and down the Thames which they might take together, to all of which Holmes promptly availed himself, with the result that, at the end of six days, both realized that they were designed for each other, and a passionate declaration followed which opened new vistas of happiness for both. Hence it was that, when the Reverend James Tattersby arrived at Goring-Streatley the following Monday night, unexpectedly, he was astounded to find sitting together in the moonlight, in the charming little English garden at the rear of his dwelling, two persons, one of whom was his daughter Marjorie and the other a young American curate to whom he had already been introduced as A. J. Raffles.

"'We have met before, I think,' said Raffles coldly, as his eye fell upon Holmes.

"'I — er — do not recall the fact,' replied Holmes, meeting the steely stare of the homecomer with one of his own flinty glances.

"'H'm!' said Raffles, nonplused at the other's failure to recognize him. Then he shivered slightly. 'Suppose we go indoors, it is a trifle chilly out here in the night air.'

"The whole thing, the greeting, the meeting, Holmes's demeanor and all, was so admirably handled that Marjorie Tattersby never guessed the truth, never even suspected the intense dramatic quality of the scene she had just gazed upon.

"'Yes, let us go indoors,' she acquiesced. 'Mr. Dutton has something to say to you, Papa.'

"'So I presumed,' said Raffles dryly. 'And something that were better said to me alone, I fancy, eh?' he added.

"'Quite so,' said Holmes calmly. And indoors they went. Marjorie immediately retired to the drawing room, and Holmes and Raffles went at once to Tattersby's study.

"'Well?' said Raffles impatiently when they were seated. 'I suppose you have come to get the Dorrington seal, Mr. Holmes.'

"'Ah — you know me, then, Mr. Raffles?' said Holmes with a pleasant smile.

"'Perfectly,' said Raffles. 'I knew you at Dorrington Hall the moment I set eyes on you and, if I hadn't, I should have known later, for the night after your departure Lord Dorrington took me into his confidence and revealed your identity to me.'

"'I am glad,' said Holmes. 'It saves me a great deal of unnecessary explanation. If you admit that you have the seal —'

"'But I don't,' said Raffles. 'I mentioned it a moment ago, because Dorrington told me that was what you were after. I haven't got it, Mr. Holmes.'

"'I know that.' observed Holmes, quietly. 'It is in the possession of Miss Tattersby, your daughter, Mr. Raffles.'

"'She showed it to you, eh?' demanded Raffles, paling.

"'No. She sealed a note to me with it, however,' Holmes replied.

"'A note to you?' cried Raffles.

"'Yes. One asking for my autograph. I have it in my possession,' said Holmes.

"'And how do you know that she is the person from whom that note really came?' Raffles asked.

"'Because I have seen the autograph which was sent in response to that request in your daughter's collection, Mr. Raffles,' said Holmes.

"'So that you conclude —?' Raffles put in hoarsely.

"'I do not conclude; I begin by surmising, sir, that the missing seal of Lord Dorrington was stolen by one of two persons — yourself or Miss Marjorie Tattersby,' said Holmes, calmly.

"'Sir!' roared Raffles, springing to his feet menacingly.

"'Sit down, please,' said Holmes. 'You did not let me finish. I was going to add, Dr. Tattersby, that a week's acquaintance with that lovely woman, a full knowledge of her peculiarly exalted character and guileless nature, makes the alternative of guilt that affects her integrity clearly preposterous, which, by a very simple process of elimination, fastens the guilt, beyond all peradventure, on your shoulders. At any rate, the presence of the seal in this house will involve you in difficult explanations. Why is it here? How did it come here? Why are you known as the Reverend James Tattersby, the missionary, at Goring-Streatley, and as Mr. A. J. Raffles, the cricketer and man of the world, at Dorrington Hall, to say nothing of the Cliveden plate —'

"'Damnation!' roared the Reverend James Tattersby again, springing to his feet and glancing instinctively at the long low bookshelves behind him.

"'To say nothing,' continued Holmes, calmly lighting a cigarette, 'of the Cliveden plate now lying concealed behind those dusty theological tomes of yours which you never allow to be touched by any other hand than your own.'

"'How did you know?' cried Raffles.

"'I didn't,' laughed Holmes. 'You have only this moment informed me of the fact!'

"There was a long pause, during which Raffles paced the floor like a caged tiger.

"'I'm a dangerous man to trifle with, Mr. Holmes,' he said finally. 'I can shoot you down in cold blood in a second.'

"'Very likely,' said Holmes. 'But you won't. It would add to the difficulties in which the Reverend James Tattersby is already deeply immersed. Your troubles are sufficient, as matters stand, without your having to explain to the world why you have killed a defenseless guest in your own study in cold blood.'

"'Well — what do you propose to do?' demanded Raffles, after another pause.

"'Marry your daughter, Mr. Raffles, or Tattersby, whatever your permanent name is — I guess it's Tattersby in this case,' said Holmes. 'I love her and she loves me. Perhaps I should apologize for having wooed and won her without due notice to you, but you doubtless will forgive that. It's a little formality you sometimes overlook yourself when you happen to want something that belongs to somebody else.'

"What Raffles would have answered no one knows. He had no chance to reply, for at that moment Marjorie herself put her radiantly lovely little head in at the door with a 'May I come in?' and a moment later she was gathered in Holmes's arms, and the happy lovers received the Reverend James Tattersby's blessing. They were married a week later and, as far as the world is concerned, the mystery of the Dorrington seal and that of the Cliveden plate was never solved.

"'It is compounding a felony, Raffles,' said Holmes,

after the wedding, 'but for a wife like that, hanged if I wouldn't compound the ten commandments!'

"I hope," I ventured to put in at that point, "that the marriage ceremony was not performed by the Reverend James Tattersby."

"Not on your life!" retorted Raffles Holmes. "My father was too fond of my mother to permit of any flaw in his title. A year later I was born, and — well, here I am — son of one, grandson of the other, with hereditary traits from both strongly developed and ready for business. I want a literary partner — a man who will write me up as Bunny did Raffles, and Watson did Holmes, so that I may get a percentage on that part of the swag. I offer you the job, Jenkins. Those royalty statements show me that you are the man, and your books prove to me that you need a few fresh ideas. Come, what do you say? Will you do it?"

"My boy," said I, enthusiastically, "don't say another word. Will I? Well, just try me!"

And so it was that Raffles Holmes and I struck a bargain and became partners.